Copyright © 2021 Erin Graves

ISBN: 9798759250043

All rights reserved. No part of this publication may be reproduced, distributed, or transmitted in any form or by any means, including photocopying, recording, or other electronic or mechanical methods, without the prior written permission of the publisher, except in the case of brief quotations embodied in critical reviews and certain other noncommercial uses permitted by copyright law.

It's Christmas time at our house,
and you know what that means.
Kitty thinks she gets to play with all
the Christmas things.

She thinks the decorations
and lights are all for her.
When I warn her not to touch them
she just flicks her tail and purrs.

Our tree is up, the lights are on,
everything's just right.
But Kitty thinks it's her playground
to climb on day and night.

We have to hide our presents.
They can't stay under the tree.
If there is even one left out,
Kitty opens them quickly.

If Kitty wants to find a place
to take a little nap,
she climbs into my stocking,
not onto my lap.

She usually gets stuck
and then she starts to pout.
When I hear her little meows
I rescue her and pull her out.

Silent Cat
Ho Ho Ho Kitty Cat
Kitty Christmas Stories

Hot cocoa is not for cats,
but Kitty doesn't know.
When it cools down she takes small sips
and nibbles marshmallows.

Sometimes Kitty thinks
the ornaments are her toys.
Anything she gets her paws on,
she usually destroys.

If it's shiny or it jingles,
Kitty wants to play.
It's a miracle if there
are any left on Christmas Day.

Days Until Christmas

1 2

"Uh-oh Kitty, you're all tied up.
You've really done it now.
We are going to have to untangle you,
but I'm not quite sure how.

First, hold very still.
Then turn this way and that.
Now you're free to play again
my silly Christmas cat."

I keep my eye on Kitty
when I'm having my Christmas treat.
If I want to eat my cookies
I can't let her steal my seat.

"Kitty, you took that shining star right off of our Christmas tree! If you want to be on the Nice List, you better give that back to me!"

It's Christmas Eve and Kitty's tired.
She's had a busy holiday.
A day of fun and mischief
with another on the way.

She sleeps with one eye open
so she doesn't miss a thing.
She's heard about the magic
that Christmas night can bring.

Goodnight Kitty.

What do YOU think Kitty will get into on Christmas Day?

Kitty Loves
Christmas

Made in the USA
Columbia, SC
10 December 2024

48981559R00015